The Missions of Gulls

including

The Ballad of Sally Stardust

and

Other Space Junk

Copyright © 2022 Ted Lamb
Illustrations: Shutterstock Images

E-mail: tedlambbooks@yahoo.com
Tel: 07388 158316

No material from this work may be reproduced without prior permission from the author.

The Missions of Gulls

and other verses

Ted Lamb

For Caspar and Sarah

The Missions of Gulls

I'd like to sit here on the cliff
and ponder the missions of seagulls
as they cross and recross this scene.
But you would rather roll on your back
and squint at the sky so high, so high
and wonder where it ends.

Look, three are crossing the azure bay below
measured and purposeful: their aim?
Are they bound for France, perhaps? Cadiz?
Don't you want to know their game?

Your face tells nothing, just a sunkissed smile
amid the sea pinks and the thymey turf
washed with scented air as we are lulled
by the sleepy draws of the surf.

Happy Homesteaders

Oh, to lie back on my childhood bed again,
and dream contented for a little while
listening to fledglings whispering in the roof,
the scrape of tiny feet on summer tiles.
Lazy bird-chat on warm air
stirs memories of long ago
A house with nesting sparrows is a happy house
as anyone so blessed will tell you so.

Unofficial Ambassadors

*It's said they're Londoners through and through
black-bibbed, the cock is every inch a Cockney, neat
head on one side, bright eye on you
pecking at crumbs around your feet.*

*And often, in some far-off place
the little dandies and their smart grey wives
gather about you when you sit
and ask you very sweetly for baksheesh.*

The Beau of Spring

The orchard's blessed:
A boastful puffed out chest
of rarest blushing pink...
the bullfinch beau is back in bloom
after his long grey winter test.

Dressed to kill, and though a menace to your fruit
you can forgive the blossom's ruin
and surely miss a plum or two
for just a glimpse of that romantic suit.

An Understanding with Ravens

The watchers in the sentinel pine that tops the ridge
are friends of mine. They call as I approach.
I answer and we play our counting game
- sharp as razors, they will not give in
'til we are up to seven croaks.

Then, patience lost, they swoop
and circle slowly overhead
calling me to follow and fly upside-down like them,
then laughing at my anchored feet.

At last they reel away, abandoned to the gale
"I bet you can't do this," their parting jeer.
I must admit it's bloody neat.

The Clever Gulls of Amsterdam

*The clever gulls in Amsterdam
keep treading up and down
a score or more are marking time
and puzzling the town.
Is it a game, this marching craze,
this avian intrigue?
Or maybe some quaint custom
of the Hanseatic League?
No. The worms are deep, and only rain
can lure the squiggly dinners up again
...or maybe something like the sound
of raindrops pitter-patter
on the gull-fandangoed ground...*

The Gathering of the Clans

*We'd walked many long miles, she and I
dropping down into a deep Cantabrian valley
cradling a vast brown sleeping monastery.*

*Exhausted, we sat outside a cafe
drinking cappuccinos and the scene,
the air like wine
in probably the last warmth of autumn
and talking of reaching Santiago far away.*

*In a magic moment, from every direction
the martins from all Europe
descended in a snowstorm
to wheel around the turreted cloister walls
thousands upon thousands
a galaxy of twinkling stars.*

*Spellbound and speechless
we listened to their gossip...
'Hello! And how was your summer in the Alps?
Or in Berlin? Or Gloucestershire?'*

*And then, as if at some signal, the great cloud
lifted, a noisy cartwheel, ready to depart.
And we looked at each other, she and I
each with this single thought
(because, on the Camino, you think
such things, you know):
'Maybe God meant us to be here for this
...and we've been blessed to share it so .'*

Midnight Serenade

*My 20th year. March. The lane is dark and long
the overcast obliterating stars
my last lift many hours ago
nothing to do but trudge, no hope of cars.
The coast of Spain is many leagues away
and here, benighted, I am still in France
my love is waiting by the sea
... but all at once I stop, entranced
by golden notes from the tall, black hedge
wraith birds ... not one, or two or three, far more
all pouring out their hearts
all singing from the same enchanted score.
Nightingales in passage. What a joy!
Of all places, it is here we've crossed
to share this tumult of crescendos
while back in England I have left sharp frost.
Where are they bound I wonder?
To Holland? Vaihingen? Or Highnam Woods?
And who can be blessed with such a happy heart
as all too soon we take our separate roads.*

The Pheasant King

Kakaaarkcha! Kakaaarkcha! Who dares to challenge me,
the monarch of the lawn - Kakaaarkcha! Heed you
my regal strut and fine proud chest
my peaked crown, spurred heels
a haughty yellow eye set in a crimson cheek,
white collar, cape of shimmering green
and cloak of glittering bronze-gold mail
that rattles fearsome as I throw my head up high and cry
Kakaaarkcha!
and sweep my fine barred train along the dew.

The Wagtail's Friend

Where are you now, John Clare?
Looking down with kindly eye I hope
on wagtails trotting by the brook
happy at last with friends of old,
fellows and maids you loved and laughed with
before your life grew difficult and cold.
I feel I know you. If only we could meet, and run,
chase moorhens splashing up some rushy stream,
laugh in the innocent delights of April sun.

Two for Joy

One for sorrow, two for joy
three for a girl, four for a boy
five for silver, six for gold
seven for a tale that's never been told.
And eight for...what? Two boys, maybe
and nine, perhaps three girls
and ten, more silver coins to count?
Eleven? All that rhymes is 'pearls'
twelve is easy - yet more gold
at thirteen, boundless woes unfold
unless you tip your hat and say
a hasty thirteenfold g'day!
I would go further, but I'm stuck
fourteen's where a mother magpie
(or indeed a mother duck)
requires a large amount of luck.

Tumblefalling

*The raggedy rooks are tumblefalling
spinning to earth in noisy pairs
above is a circling audience, cawing,
applauding every giddy feat with cheers.
In the piled white clouds and blue blue sky of March
abandoned to the rushing air they spiral down
pulling out, triumphant, just short of crashing
flat in a new-sprung field of emerald corn.
The heart beats faster. Listen, look,
It's surely spring again. And the waking earth
bids souls to tumble with the rooks,
and dance for the glory of rebirth.*

I Remember Blakeney

*I sat outside my cottage,
and, closing my eyes, slowly became aware
of a blackbird's song.
Troubled thoughts dissolved,
of war and rumours wracking all the world,
replaced by the balm of orchard notes,
cadences and pauses, pitched at the sun,
phrases pouring loud and soft
dropping through clear spring air like liquid gold.
And I thought of a soldier poet
in a sidelined train so very long ago
whose war was for a beat forgotten
when a blackbird sang in Adelstrop
as his engine waited, idling,
and he longed it not to go.*

Car Park Aldermen

Statesmanlike, with a corporation waddle,
alderman rooks explore a plastic cup, move on
inspect chip paper and a Big Mac wrapper
gravely pacing twixt Land Rover and Citroen.

The Last Shot

*Eleven, and as sure a shot with airgun
as you have ever seen;
rabbits, starlings, even pretty songbirds
a challenge to my aim.
And then, one bright, bright summer day
three chattering jackdaws flew above, quite high
and shooting from the hip, unthinking
I dropped one from the sky.
It tumbled like a falling rag
and I rushed to claim my prize
across the stubble field, to stand
just as life left its blue-grey eye.
But the crimson blood on black
and the golden stalks
brought not triumph, only shame;
why oh why had I made killing
into such a wanton game?
That life, so careless-wasted
meant I never shot again.*

Swan Majesty

*Nothing so glorious as swans in flight
a vision heard as much as seen
as every long, strong quill is bent
to drive majestic shapes of purest white.*

*Nothing so wonderful as swans a-sail
with wings upstretched and scooping air
and heads held high and proud
to scud along black waters in a gale.*

*Nothing so at peace as swans asleep
heads under wings and rocking gently on the waves
 dreaming of we know not what
while all extremeties are tucked in neat.*

Dandenong Chimes

We loved to walk amid the tall cool trees
along the shimmering ridge above the baking plain
rosellas a startle of colour on the picnic tables
and Dandenong bellbirds ringing
in the crisp blue eucalypt air, unseen.
A memory to treasure when I'm low
and England's wrapped in bitter winter rain
and she who shared the bellbirds' chimes
can never share with me again.

Night Companions

*How comforting to walk in the dark in the company of owls
answering back to that tremulous whoo-hooo
imagining their astonished tawny faces
puzzled by a wanderer's incomprehensible howls.*

*Often, on some lonely roadway through deep woods
such night companionship has cheered me on
making the footsteps lighter over passing miles
as nighttime fears dissolve in owly singalongs.*

Waking Company

*Israel, 1969. Warm, and I'd slept out in the cool
waking to find my bones protesting in a heavy dew
while near me pecked a rosy, busy early riser
flicking a chequered crest, making no move to go.
The friendly bird they call it - in those old books of long
ago
hoopoes would follow the wandering tribe
fleeing from oppression, companions in the desert dust
seeking with them a promised land, a place to grow.
My sitting and yawning was too much and off it flew
on zebra wings, looping from the kibbutz lawn
trailing a plaintive note I would forever know
in the growing heat of a blazing Palestine dawn.*

A Winter's Tale

*Christmas, 1980, Toorak - a barbie in the sun
and inside on the sideboard, greetings cards aglow
with holly, jolly carol singers, village scenes,
trees glittering with baubles - and robins in the snow.
Only a year ago we cursed and took a sledge
to trudge through melted sludge for sacks of coal
and along that English road the only festive cheer
a robin singing bravely in the hedge.
Most Melbournites will never know
how sweet this winter caroller sounds to chilblained ears
or quite how startling its red breast can be
while winter's grip is monochrome and sere.*

Late spring 2013

Spring had forgotten the forest;
April bleak as January
forbade the bluebell shoots to show
and locked the buds of oak and ash
while grey skies threatened snow.
Yet from the frost-browned thicket
one voice came loud and clear
the tiniest of birds, a wren,
undaunted chanticleer.

Sparrowhawk

Sudden assassin, a shocking thing
almost air itself,
a slate-grey blurr with sickle claws,
sting-pointed, primed to reach and snatch
jinking out of nowhere into nowhere in a blink
leaving a thud in the brain
a sudden silence just above the lawn,
a wisp of bloodied down,
nothing.

Eleonora's Falcon

Heat blazed from forbidding cliffs
barring our way ahead on that Agean isle
searching for a rumoured pass
to the old white temple perched above the pile.
No way seemed open - then the guardians of the rocks
set upon us, screaming pain
flapping hard wings in our faces,
harpies of the heights
turning in a beat to soar again,
mere dots in the stratosphere
and before we'd caught our breath
more metal bolts than birds,
back at our heads, their message clear:
Turn around at once, and stay away from here!

Waking Call

'This song's for you, for you, for you. You',
the pigeon croons through mists of morning sleep
a comforter in the glorious dawn
to wake me up to think,
'This song's for you, for you, for you. You,
There's things to do, to do, to do'.

Birds Elemental

*Piping of curlews winging through the night
on a wild sky, sketched against the moon
Sounds and sights to raise the spirits high
and make my way more lightly through the gloom.*

*Arrow-swift the little flock scuds by
bound for black moorland far away from town
trailing their plaintive wails along the wind
birds elemental to folk spooked in bed and gown.*

*"Hark! It's the Seven Sisters - they bode ill"
once was the fear of narrow minds -
but not for me, remembering still
untrammeled wonder in those windswept sounds.*

More Poems

Haymaking

*Tractors snarl around the fields
where once our patient ponies trod
to save the hay;
for horses, a week's work at least
that now takes but a day
for young men, earphones clamped
to heads
listening to some zombie rap;
cutting the fragrant grasses low
to chop, ensile and put away
quite mindlessly.*

*I'd give up what's left of my time
to sail once more a boy, with friends
like Peter Knapp, and giggling Annie R,
high aboard the haywain, down the lane
touching hedges on each side
while mirth takes all our breath away.*

The Mermaid

In a tangle of rope and wrack and foam
I found the mermaid
combing her hair.
'Quickly, into the sea', said she.

I could not resist
and so we played all day
at catching her tail
and sometimes she let me win...

Later we parted, tired and happy
and off I went home to another.
'And where have you been all the day?'
said she.

The Witch Pool

Dark the pool where mosses grow
Dip toe, dip toe,
Silent, cool? It's always so
until the sun goes down...

Then, round the pool where mosses grow
– pool, moss, moon glow –
from the shadows, starting slow
one by one the witches go.

Then round and round the pool they go.
Ever faster round they go
round the pool where mosses grow
round and round and round.

Heel for heel and toe for toe
more and more now, row on row
round and round the witches go
round and round and round.

Faster, leaping, crouching low
wailing, shrieking! On they go
underneath the moon oh
underneath the moon
round the pool where mosses grow,
round and round and round
whirling, twirling on they go
faster, wilder! Round and round...
until the moon sinks low ...

*Slow then, slower, ever slow
round still go the witches oh
until the dawn begins to glow.*

*Then shadows into shadows go
by the pool where mosses grow.*

*Dip toe, dip toe,
dark the pool where mosses grow.*

Forest Farewell

My neighbour Hilda went to rest
familiar folk around on bended knee
as in the little Forest church
she took the path we all must take
into eternity.

I never knew her all that well
but sometimes, walking in the lanes
I'd heard he singing as gran used to do
old songs, and snatches from her childhood games.

And as the priest read of her life
as hard a time as could be lived on earth,
we stood together, quiet, and wept
and not a soul could ever doubt her worth.

I felt she stood there with us as we sang
How Great Thou Art, and said our last goodbye
and laughed to cheer us as we all filed out
to shake hands under the leaden winter sky.

The shuffled feet, the hard-wrung smiles
showed all knew not so many miles
lay on our own path through the trees
to the lights at last of home.

The Summary of Years

*It is not hard to percieve age as a curse,
made as we are from mere sub-particles,
formed as the sea takes sand and casts it on the shore,
briefly creating the semblance of a being
trapped amid these boundless stars by bathetic ignorance,
remembering, forgetting,
reaching, touching, missing.
Imagining we will find.
Surer often we will lose.
Let alone the other accumulating ills,
the failing,
the fearing,
the falling,
impending witlessness,
a wispy nothing, vanishing like the curl of a wave.*

*Yet, in a long life, remember,
weren't there as many goods as ills,
wonders, surprises, joys?
Sufficient unto the day the fingerholds of comfort?
So it must always be: the future is never to be feared.
We are still more than the sum of the whole
have soared above once-perceived limits
and look to soar yet higher.
The grail we seek lies
far beyond the visible and known.
and yet the call to know is strong
for everyone, but all the same our own.*

*So do not read here a complaint.
If there is nothing, why do we still seek?
Raise yourself from the earth
escape the ties of ground,
surf on for the truths that are not yet found
and discover rights for wrongs,
new healing for old ills,
justice and peace and love,
and our unknown destiny.*

Whale song

*The whale was singing
"I love you, I love you, I love you"
to the men on the boat
when the harpoon struck.
She was dead even as she sounded
trailing her crimson blood
and its dark scent
through jade waves down to
obsidian depths
that once spelled sanctuary.*

*Beyond the flensing
and the rendering
the men saw
bright lights in Albany;
a new dress for Molly;
and cash in hand to buy fine tea.*

The Eagle and the Lambs

The eagle's on the lambs again!
And people rush with pots and pans
To clash and shout and make loud bangs
To keep the eagle off the lambs.

The Chemistry of Love

She said, 'It isn't really love
unless you're very stupid.
See, chemistry's behind it all.
What makes you think it's Cupid?
It's horny moans and fairy moans
that activate erogenous zones
for all the boys, testoblerone,
Easter again for girls.'

Infinity

Let the race to space go on apace
I for one don't like it
It's big and old and dark and cold
And can't be nice as my bit.

The Ballad of Sally Stardust
and Other Space Junk

The Ballad of Sally Stardust

*When they hear a tapping in the starship bulkheads
stirring settler babies in the hiber-bays,
"Hush," croon the nurse-tones
"It's only Sally Stardust,
Searching for her lover down the space highways."*

*She was just a singer in an outpost clip joint
When the handsome stranger came into her life
For a night she held him
Then he had to ship out
Running, never stopping, running for his life.*

*Sally stole a cruiser from the deep space park-lot
Blasted from the shadows of the moon's dark side
Bad-fingered the cop-ships
Lined up a star chart
Crashed the screaming engines into hyperdrive.*

*Some say Sally's lover was a gambler and a killer
Others just a victim, framed and without vice
Sally only knew him
As a lucked-out loner
Knew she had to follow in his endless flight.*

*Now she roams the space lanes, singing like an angel
Making a living while she keeps her hopes alive
She will never stay much
longer than an eye-blink
Moving on as swiftly as she first arrived.*

Always just behind her lurk the silent watchers
Hoping she will lead them where her man can't hide
She can feel their presence
Dark and cold and evil
Knows she must outrun them or her sweetheart dies.

Sally is a legend wherever there are roamers
The story of her love has travelled far and wide
And some say she's still out there
Moving on forever
Driven by the fire of a love that never dies.

When a shooting star flares brightly in the twilight,
Mothers tell their children not to be afraid,
"See, it's Sally Stardust
Poor, lost Sally Stardust
Doomed to keep on searching til the end of days."

Someday you may see her, listen to her sweet voice
When you break your journey in some far rest bay.
You will know it's Sally,
eyes so deep with sadness
But before the spell ends she'll be on her way.

Then, if strangers ask you if ever you saw her,
Say 'someone like her, but with different eyes,
An ordinary bar girl,
An ordinary singer.'
And she never, never told you where her destination lies.

Maybe she has found him, shaking off the watchers
Maybe in some far world they are in each others' arms
Hidden from the stalkers
Free at last from worries
Happy now together, safe at last from harm.

Eldorado

*From the observation deck, standing off
we at last beheld Auris,
planet of purest gold
and marvelled.*

*Her shining sterile face
so beautiful
so deadly,
the Midas curse her worth
in unattainable wealth -
all who landed,
(and there were many who tried)
trapped by her immense density
along with their desires
and burned at once to vapour
under her merciless skies.*

The Universal Wrench

*On a planet (not unlike our earth maybe,
Or then again, perhaps not)
Far, far away (or nearer)
Sometime (or almost any day)
You will find someone using
A universal wrench.
And (perhaps with a hint of surprise)
You will say
"Aha! You have those too!"
And they will say (surprised)
"Of course we do."
And then you'll say
"And what do you call it?"
And they (or perhaps your translator)
Will say:
"A universal wrench of course. What else?"
And you will realise
That far into the past, and in the future
As today,
The universal wrench has always been
And so will stay
The tool that fixed the universe (perhaps)
Which (if it did not already exist,
Like the wheel and other deities
that are inherently adjustable)
Would have to be invented.*

Luna

*Luna. You'd think she would be ugly
being so very old
But no; she still comes up shining
and on her face that giaconda smile.*

*Just as - oh, many years ago
she shone on dewy gossamer-strung silver meadows
while I sped along the lovely, lonely night road
from Oxford to Swindon
piston slap ricocheting
off the May hedges,
just as she glowed, huge and rosy
through harvest dust
while I discovered lust.*

*Still she shines and smiles
on the care worn
on the war torn
on the obscenely rich
and on the poor.*

*It takes her 28 years
to wander back to the same spot again
by which time everyone has forgotten
where it was she started. Three chances
perhaps in a lifetime
to see her just so; just as well our memories
aren't that long.*

*Luna, luna, luna
smiling, shining
for the lover*

for the lunatic
for the murderer
for the saint
for me
for you.

The Day Trippers

They wandered down a wormhole
to Winchester one day
Little green men in straw hats
breezy, spruce and gay.

Warping out of subspace
they drove up to an inn
parked the ship on yellow lines
and merrily went on in.

They drank some beers
they pinched the girls
'til the landlord came to say
'I'm glad you're 'avin fun, my lads
now which of you's going to pay?'

They zapped the town
and burned it down
but kept postcards to show
that life on earth can be full of mirth
if ever you want to go.

Real Estate

*The universe, everything, space
to be serious
is yours and mine and nobody's.
But someone, sometime, somewhere
will parcel
bits of it up and sell it off
lot by lot, as real estate
you wait and see.
Maybe they already have.
Maybe we are all on someone's
building plot
maybe, maybe, maybe
(try selling this concept to the guys
who think they own Park Lane).*

More than words

*In the tilt and tumble
of passing days,
old stones grow older, yet
deep in their density hold
the overheard echoes of
our words,
sinking in from the beginning;
loves, hates, sweet nothings
promises and lies are
all stored up within.*

*And our infant cries still
fly out forever through earth's circling void,
our adult declarations follow,
travelling ever on.
Words. Seemingly loose, random
a jumble not connecting.
Only sometimes can we catch them
and hold on.*

The Song of the Earth

*All was black before the raven said
in his terrible big voice, 'Awake!'
And the deep dark valleys
and the black, black hills
rang with the awful awsome sound.*

*And, slowly, slowly, over the rim of the world
came the red light of the sun –
a glow, then bigger, bigger, bigger still.
The blackbird poured a jewelled song
and the kookaburra added
'Oh, ha. Oh ha, oh ha ha ha ha ha!'
and the lark joined in, 'I must get higher,
higher and I will, I will, I will!'
and all the birds from near and far
joined in and sang to the sun
with their little hearts on fire.*

*And creatures, one by one awoke,
and smiled, and they sang too
the bear, the sloth and the kangaroo
all sang with a great and joyous noise
waking the grownups, the girls and boys,
the babies, old mothers with their sticks
and ancient men on ricketty legs –
the good, the bad, and yes, the ugly too,
stirred, then threw their windows wide
and heard it all, and saw
the laughing dewy faces of the flowers,
and drank in gladness and goodwill.*

And the raven spoke again:
'Let there now be no more ills!'
And the earth turned, and
every one and every thing turned with it
happily through sunny starry space
and there was never more any wrong.

THE END

You might also enjoy other books by *Ted Lamb...

Surge! (Kindle E-book, paperback) In a re-run of a tragic historical flood, the west coast of Britain faces an unstoppable fury.
Match of the Day (Kindle E-book) Remember Britain's 1960 Football World Cup campaign? A bitter-sweet coming-of-age story.
Gansalaman's Gold (Kindle E-book) Fancy a transylvanian holiday? Strange disappearances in Dracula country.
Brassribs (Kindle E-book, paperback) Two generations of anglers have sought Brightwell Lake's biggest carp – but the book also tells of wartime bravery, romance and skulduggery.
Looking for Lucie (Kindle E-book, paperback) Lucie is a very, very big pike – yet while fanatical angler Mark Kendal is trying to catch her, his world is falling apart. What happens when the adversaries finally meet?
Gobblemouth (Kindle E-book, paperback) A problem catfish that has to be rehomed is behind this madcap road-trip across Europe to the River Danube.
The Brightwell Trilogy (Kindle E-book, paperback) The above three books – **Brassribs**, **Looking for Lucie** and **Gobblemouth** – are contained in this bumper edition.
One Last Cast: reflections on a fishing life (poetry on Kindle E-book, paperback).
The Fisher's Tale (Kindle E-book, paperback) Walking the pilgrim trail from France to Spain's Santiago de Compostela in 2003.
*Ted Lamb has been a writer and journalist in Britain and Australia all his working life and his books reflect a keen interest in sport fishing, natural history and travel. He lives in Cheltenham, England.